I'd like to dedicate this little tale to my mum… You've always been my biggest supporter, and you're the greatest one-woman cheer squad anyone could ever wish for. I love you. Thank you for standing by me, and helping me out with the little ones while I chase my dream!

x

Zoey, July 2020

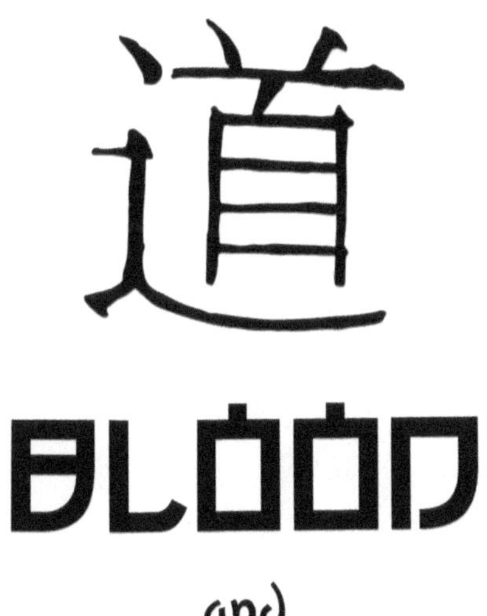

BLOOD
and
SILK

ZOEY XOLTON

Takashi leaned down to kiss his mother farewell. Already he could see worry lines etched into the corners of her intelligent and kind eyes. Bright streaks of silver peppered her long locks of ebony, though it did little to detract from her austere beauty. She was a small woman, but fierce in her love, and loyal to a fault.

At eighteen years of age, Takashi yearned to

leave the peace and safety of their small country village to travel far into the mountains and beyond, in search of adventure, and a wife. While his elder brothers worked the farm out of duty—their father having died two winters past—he was not burdened by such obligations. A seventh son was a blessing, and as was tradition in Edo period Japan, his birthright was the freedom to decide his own fate.

His mother wanted him to experience the world, educate himself, and find a good woman with whom he could grow a family. She feared for him, but that was only natural. He was her favourite; fairer by far than his six brothers. She told him often that he belonged to the farm no more than a peacock to the mire. As a peacock's beauty was to be admired, at home within the palace gardens of the Emperor, he too was destined for a life far more splendid than any she could provide for him. He was her golden child, her lucky child.

"Have courage, be kind, and wear our family name with honour," she said, stoically holding back her tears. "And beware the yōkai in the mountains. They are beautiful, mischievous, and often calamitous creatures…and those that dwell there are old beyond memory. They have lured many an unsuspecting traveller to their doom. Be smart and stay on the path, my son, and all should be well."

Takashi gently untangled his hands from his mother's, petting hers in a final gesture of comfort. "I will return, Mother, you have my word. No yōkai could keep me from you. The blessings of our ancestors are with me, I feel it."

Kaori pursed her lips and swallowed her fears. "I trust in your promise, Takashi. May the light of Amaterasu shine down upon you, and keep you safe, even when the road is dark. Now go, before I lose my nerve and the day is lost!"

Takashi bowed low to his mother before

collecting his pack and setting off with a wave.

Kaori stood by the front door of their humble, thatched home long after she lost sight of her son. "Good fortune be with you, my son," she whispered, her simple prayer born swiftly away on the morning breeze. *His fate was his own now.*

14

Revelling in the fragrant scent of the blushing pink sakura blossoms, and the clean mountain air, Takashi stepped lightly, his hopes and mood high. The cloudless blue sky, the steady drone of the busy bees, and the wafting clouds of colourful, dancing butterflies were all good omens. *How lucky am I, that I should be born a seventh son?* he thought. *I am truly free to pursue my dreams, and my future is my own*

to shape and mould as I will! He felt the very joy of life bubbling within him and he smiled freely, humming a cheerful tune as he walked.

By noon his legs were beginning to feel the rigour of the climb. Trekking a while further, he came upon a peaceful, secluded lake by which he could relax and stretch his sore limbs. Setting down his pack, he cupped his hands and drank of the lake's cool, pure waters, his long tail of hair falling over his shoulder. Splashing his face, he rubbed his eyes to clear them. When next he looked up, he startled, catching his breath. Across the small lake was a young maiden of ethereal beauty.

Even from a distance, there was no mistaking how exquisite she was. Unlike most women of the Orient, her eyes were a magnificent bright and piercing blue; the colour he imagined sapphires might be. Her long locks of black hung free to her waist, several lengths plaited and interwoven with traditional ornaments of jade and silver; and upon her head she wore a wreath of fragrant mountain flowers. With the golden light of the afternoon sun behind her, she was surely every bit as majestic as the Queen of Heaven, herself.

Rising to his feet, Takashi wiped his hands on his maroon robes. "Konichiwa," he called in greeting, not wanting to frighten the young woman. "I did not see you there!"

The maiden smiled in response, inclining her head ever so slightly, causing the decorations in her hair to jingle. "Would you join me for refreshments?" she called.

Takashi vibrated with nervous excitement. He had never been invited to keep the company of a woman, before. Such things were usually restricted until courtship. He smiled broadly in response and hurriedly collected his belongings. Skirting the lake, he plucked a stunning indigo waterlily from the lake's edge, sparing the winding mountain path only a fleeting glance as he left it behind.

"Konichiwa," said the maiden as he approached. "Would you share in my bounty? I have sweet, fresh peaches, crisp pears, and a gourd of homemade wine. I'd be glad for the company."

"It would be my honour, thank you," said Takashi with a bow.

The maiden sank elegantly to her knees, her ornate ivory-white kimono pooling around her. Takashi sat a respectable distance away so as not to offend or assume familiarity.

"What do they call you, friend?" she asked, as she pared the fruit with a small gemstone encrusted knife.

"My name is Takashi, son of Rajin Hiroto. And what may I call you, my lady?"

"Your father was named for the god of thunder? A powerful name, indeed."

Takashi smiled in acknowledgement before popping a slice of juicy fruit into his mouth.

"I am called Shiori," his companion continued. "And am no lady. I am a Silk Maiden."

Takashi's brow furrowed. "Forgive me, but I am not familiar with such a title. Do you sell silk? I see your garment is of great splendour. The embroidery is intricate, and truly beautiful to behold—such a gown would befit the empress, herself! Did you make it?"

Shiori's jewel-toned eyes regarded him thoughtfully. "I thank you for your praise," she said, sipping from the gourd. "I do make my own silk."

"Such talent! It must take great skill, and many hours to create attire such as this. You are certainly a master of the loom."

A pleasant rosy colour flushed Shiori's cheek, and she coyly dropped her eyes. "It is all I have ever known," she confessed. "I have spun and woven silk for as long as I can remember."

"I see," said Takashi, taking a generous draught from the gourd when it was passed. "A family trade, then?"

Shiori smiled. "You could say that."

"I know all about that," said Takashi emphatically. "I was born to a family of farmers—men of the land for generations. I am only here today because my mother bid me to explore and see the world before it comes time for me to settle and start a family of my own."

"So, this is your first journey to Mount Fuji, Takashi? Does it please you?"

"It is, and so far, I am more than impressed. The mountain is very different to the fields of the village where I grew up. It's breath-taking. From your evident comfort here, may I assume that this is not your first journey into the mountains, Shiori?"

The Silk Maiden laughed, the sound like

enchanting music to his ears. "I live here," she said simply. "And I have never ventured far. I have never had the need, to be honest."

Takashi looked around as he continued to eat and drink his fill. "Is there a village nearby, then?" he asked. "I had no idea! I thought the Shinto monastery was the first settlement along the path?"

Shiori leaned forward in a conspiratorial manner, her alluring painted red lips mere inches from his ear. "It is a hidden village, well off the path. Few know of its existence. In fact, it cannot be found, except by those who already know the way."

Takashi's skin thrummed with warmth from the wine, and his eyes lit instantly with excitement.

"Oh, I should not have said!" the Silk Maiden suddenly lamented, recoiling. "What a fool I am, revealing such things to a traveller I have only just met! I am afraid to admit, your charm has caught me quite by surprise! I am not usually so—"

Takashi sat tall, a serious expression upon his features. "You are no fool, Shiori," he interrupted. "You can trust me, you have my word. I will not share this knowledge with another soul. And it is no fault to be quick to trust. It is both noble and endearing."

Shiori sighed and visibly relaxed. The young traveller found himself glad that she took him at his word, for he meant what he said.

The Silk Maiden remained silent for a time, and together they enjoyed the rich beauty and tranquillity of the mountain and the mirror-clear lake. Spring on the mountain was nothing short of enchanting. High above the lower plains of Japan, anything seemed possible. He felt it in his bones that his destiny was somehow tied to the mountain; and he'd felt it even more acutely since the moment he'd first laid eyes on Shiori. A life of freedom and adventure felt tantalisingly within his reach, and it seemed almost too good to be true.

Shiori cleared her throat, biting her lower lip in a self-conscious manner. Takashi found this gesture delightfully becoming. Shiori was bewitching! He could barely keep his eyes off her. She seemed so pure and coy. *Obviously the result of a good and honourable upbringing*, he thought. *I'd like to meet her family*. What kind of life did they lead in the foothold of the mountain? Did she descend from a merchant family who had settled on Mount Fuji after making their fortune in the silk trade?

As if in answer to his questions, Shiori glanced at Takashi from beneath her thick, black lashes. "I am hesitant to ask this of you," she began. "You see, I've never met another that I feel this way, about. I feel—rightly or wrongly—that I can trust you. There is an integrity in you that is not often seen around these parts. The mountain can be such a dangerous place..." Tucking an errant lock of hair behind her petite ears, she smiled shyly. "Would you like to see my home, Takashi? I will understand if you consider me too forward."

"No!" exclaimed Takashi. "I mean, not at all. I am honoured by your trust. I came to Mount Fuji in search of adventure, and to experience life's many mysteries. It would be a pleasure and privilege to see your hidden village, Shiori."

The Silk Maiden rose to her feet, smoothing her elegant kimono. "Then come," she invited, her jewel-like gaze boring into his soul. "You'll have to forgive me, the way is unusual, but that is how we have managed to remain safe, and secret all these years."

"I understand," said Takashi. "Please lead the way and I will follow."

The two unlikely companions left the lakeside and ventured into the verdant forest beyond. They chatted pleasantly as they walked, sharing laughter and stories of their youth. The more time Takashi spent with Shiori, the less attention he paid to the position of the sun, and the distance they had journeyed from the path.

As the sky darkened, they broke free of the trees and came upon a deep gash in the earth, an entranceway through solid rock. Takashi stood before the opening, gazing up at the mountain face in awe. "Your home is hidden within the mountain itself?"

Shiori blushed again at his reverence. "It is."

"Incredible," Takashi breathed. "My mother would not believe it if I told her!"

"Will you join me?" asked the Silk Maiden, her voice as sweet as honeyed tea.

For the first time, Takashi felt a wave of apprehension, as if he had been lost within a pleasant dream, or had been under a spell, and was only just awakening to his senses. "Are there no torches to light the way? It seems black as night in there," he said hesitantly. "I would not see you come to harm."

Shiori laughed, her musical voice echoing into the mouth of the cavern. "Do not fear for me," she assured him. "I know the way intimately. My feet recall the way. I will not falter."

Takashi smiled in return, despite the unusual niggling sensation that silently gnawed away at his belly. Shiori reached out and took his hand in hers, and almost immediately Takashi forgot all his concerns. He had never held another woman's hand, save for his mother's. It was a familiar gesture, one of tenderness, faith and intimacy. His cheeks flared with colour and he looked away, hoping Shiori would not see. He wanted to appear a confident man—one worthy of such a beautiful and accomplished woman—not an unsure, red-faced boy.

Two tentative steps later, and they were swallowed by darkness. In the absence of sight, Takashi placed complete trust in his guide; blind admiration of her knowledge of the terrain and her courage. To think a woman came and went in a wilderness such as this, alone, beggared belief! She was, indeed, a rare and enthralling creature.

"How many are in your family?" he asked, striking up conversation again.

"Oh, many!" came her reply in the gloom, her hand softly, but firmly maintaining a hold on his.

"Brothers?" he ventured, hopefully.

"I do not have any," she said.

"Oh?" he answered, trying not to reveal his disappointment. "It will be good to speak to your father, then." He didn't know how to entertain a room full of women, if that was indeed the case. He'd grown up among six brothers.

"So, you have sisters?"

"I do have, yes. More than I can count! Though they have all left the nest to make homes of their own, of course."

Takashi nodded sagely in the dark, carefully treading behind her. "Your mother was blessed, then! If they are near to our age, I understand. There comes a time for every child to leave their family behind, and make a life of their own," he said. "It seems we have more in common than I could have guessed, for like you, I have many siblings too. Six brothers, in fact."

They continued the rest of the way in silence, the trail through the mountain becoming more perilous the deeper they ventured. Takashi stumbled, and Shiori steadied him with surprising ease. "Tread lightly, Takashi," she warned over her shoulder. "The way becomes narrower here, and more steep."

"If you can manage, so can I," said Takashi with more surety than he felt. They'd been walking in the inky blackness for so long that his nerves were beginning to rise again. "Shiori, is your village much further?" he enquired.

"We're almost there!" she sang back, squeezing his hand tightly.

Takashi sighed, relief washing over him. As the way grew narrow, Takashi found that he could reach out with his free hand and feel the cavern's walls. They were surprisingly smooth, and every so often his hand would trail through something soft, yet sticky. Before he had the time to contemplate further, the earth gave way beneath him, and Shiori's hand slipped from his grasp. He slid into the yawning maw of the darkness at an alarming rate. "Shiori!" he called out in panic. He clawed at the rock in a vain attempt to slow his rapid and chaotic descent. His stomach lurched up into his throat as he lost contact with the tunnel entirely. Soaring through the air, his terror consumed him…and then—nothing.

Takashi groaned as he regained consciousness. Pushing himself up, he found that he had landed face-first onto a hard, brittle type of earth that seemed to shift irregularly beneath his weight. Dim firelight flickered in the gloom, slowly illuminating his landing as his vision adjusted. His eyed widened and his mouth opened and closed in silent horror as he scrambled madly backward on all fours. The skulls and bones of men littered the cave floor in an immense pile upon which he was now king. Takashi tried to steady his breathing, but his heart hammered within his chest like a smith's mallet against the anvil. It seemed an exercise in futility.

And then, unbidden, his dear mother's words of wisdom came flooding back to him: "*And beware the yōkai in the mountains. They are beautiful, mischievous, and often calamitous creatures...and those that dwell there are old beyond memory. They have lured many an unsuspecting traveller to their doom. Be smart and stay on the path, my son, and all should be well.*"

"Yōkai!" Takashi breathed with sudden clarity. His beautiful, coy Silk Maiden was a yōkai. She had to be!

"You are right, Takashi," came Shiori's voice from somewhere above. "Yōkai, I am. In times gone by, my kind was known as jorōgumo."

Takashi battled to rise, and remain steady on his feet, slipping on the bones of the less fortunate. He raised his eyes slowly, and his face drained of all colour. "Silk Maiden," he uttered, his mind racing, connecting the pieces. *It all makes sense, now.*

Dangling by a strong thread of gleaming white silk, his ethereal Shiori hung. Only, she was but half a woman, her lower body replaced by a thick, quivering, gleaming abdomen, from which eight triple-jointed legs sprouted. "Jorōgumo..." he whispered, wracking his brain for the stories of old; tales told to caution and frighten children. "You are a blood-drinking spider-woman. A bakemono! A shape-changing yōkai!" he said in disbelief.

Spinning down with the grotesque elegance of a dancer, until her face was but inches from his own, the yōkai reached out and touched his face softly. "Do you find me hideous to behold, dear Takashi?" she asked.

Takashi shook his head in earnest, despite his fear. "You are as far from hideous as you were not moments ago," he said with a sincerity that only partially disturbed him. "You are, as I presumed, a unique and rare creature of terrible beauty; a true mystery of nature, a being of ancient dark magic."

The jorōgumo smiled broadly, revealing a long pair of glistening, sinister fangs. "Are you trying to flatter me, farmer's son?" she hissed, teasing him.

"I would be a great fool to think flattery could buy my freedom at this point, Shiori. You are—as my mother once told me—very old. Perhaps as old as the mountain itself. Existing for such an unfathomable amount of time surely breeds wisdom. I could not hope to trick you with mere words." Looking down at the picked-clean bones beneath his feet, he grimaced. "Though I'm sure others have tried."

Dropping down as lightly as a bird on a branch

before him, Shiori regarded him thoughtfully. "You are different from the others," she said, gesturing to the mound upon which they stood. "All were terrified. Some driven to madness or struck dead of shock at the mere sight of me. Others have tried in vain to run, while others picked up the very bones at their feet to strike me down. None have ever simply talked to me—treated me as an equal—dared to see me as anything more than a monster. You are indeed brave. Perhaps a gift passed down from your father, dear Takashi?" she mused.

Takashi's mouth quirked with the faintest of smiles. "It would be an honour to think any part of my father's legacy lives on within me," he answered. "In truth, I have never encountered a real yōkai before, however I have learned from tales passed down from generation to generation that you are to be feared. It is said that your kind want for nothing more than death and destruction...but I feel in my heart that this is not true, at least not always. Very few things in life are black or white, or as simple as the concepts of good and evil."

"To be fair," said Shiori as she grinned mischievously, tucking an errant strand of her long hair behind her ear, "I did lead you into my nest to feed upon you as I have so many others before you. But I do so with purpose!" She circled him as he remained still, regarding her evenly in return. "I am born from a legendary family, a queen of the yōkai. I am a daughter, a sister, and soon I hope to be a mother. If I do not nourish myself, I may not survive the long period that I am tethered here, guarding my nest as my children grow and hatch!"

"You desire family?" asked Takashi, his brow rising.

"Is it not natural?" Shiori retorted. "To want such a thing? I am not so different to your mortal women. I live not just to reap, but to sow! I wish to birth a mighty brood of my own… I want to nurture them, teach them all that I know, and see them leave the nest to find their own way in the world; to find their place among the realms of Man and yōkai."

"It seems you have been judged unfairly by my kind," said Takashi. "To me you are indeed just like any other living being that walks the earth. Your kind prey upon mine, but that is as nature intended it. Men prey on a great many creatures, and yet, we are not thought of as monsters. To live, one must kill. One must eat to thrive. It is the circle of life, and we all have our place in it."

Shiori ceased her stalking, folding her arms. "Indeed."

"If it is my fate to meet my demise here and now, then it seems I cannot fight it, and that it was willed by the gods, themselves. I came of my choice to this end, though I did not know it. I decided to walk this path, and I accept that. I would beg only that you would show me mercy and make it swift. No man looks forward to the hour of his death, least of all I. Though, that I get to behold such beauty—and die by it—is a small comfort."

"You do not fear me?"

"I do, but it is a fear born of reverence. You are a mystical being, and we are all equal under the mantle of Buddha's Heaven. Many men have lived to grow old, having never had an experience such as magnificent and otherworldly as this. Perhaps fate, in its own way, has been kind. As my mother's seventh son, I set out this morning to find adventure and a wife, and I can imagine no adventure more thrilling than meeting the legendary jorōgumo."

Shiori laughed, her velvet voice ringing throughout her silken nest in the earth. "A seventh son?" she asked in wonder. "It seems you are the rarer creature, Takashi. You are unlike any man I have ever known. You did not attempt to seduce, or overcome me, even though I know well that my mortal form pleases you. And now, facing impending doom, you stand tall, holding a conversation with me in my true form, dauntless and with integrity. Over the centuries I have supped upon the blood of warriors, men of faith, and kings, and none have shown as much courage as a farmer's son."

Takashi inclined his head. "I thank you. I had hoped to live a life of honour. I am proud to know I will at least die with it."

In her true form Shiori towered over him. "Close your eyes, Takashi. I have made my decision," she whispered, brushing his mussed hair aside.

Takashi held his head high and exhaled slowly. "Sayonara, Shiori," he said. Taking one last look at her lovely face, he closed his eyes and waited for the end. *I will join my father in Heaven*, he thought. He only hoped that his short and simple life would be judged fair, so that he might cross the bridge over the supernatural Sanzu River. If not, he would have to battle demons and other horrors as he tried to make the crossing by his own strength. No soul wished to swim the Sanzu. The spirit could drown and be lost, never to make it to the Otherside, doomed to be forever parted from their Ancestors.

Bracing himself, he felt Shiori's mortal arms lift and embrace him, followed by her front pair of spiders' legs. Then he felt it—though it was nothing like he expected. Soft and warm, with increasing pressure, he felt her lips pressed against his own. *A Kiss of Death*, he reasoned, as their mouths parted, and their tongues danced.

But death never came. Takashi opened his eyes to find Shiori standing before him in her naked, human form, a demure smile upon her face, the long curtain of her hair all that spared her modesty. "I do not wish to drink your precious life away, Seventh

Son" she said, touching his face tenderly. "You are truly blessed, I feel it. You are also noble and kind, brave and wise beyond your years; and dare I admit, exceedingly fair for a mortal. You are everything that I would seek in a mate."

Takashi's eyes widened in sudden understanding.

"Would you take me for your wife, dear Takashi? And raise an immortal family with me? We can live here in the mountain and explore the world together. Say 'yes' and I will gift you an eternal life, all the worldly treasures I possess, and, if you so desire it…my heart."

"You can make me into a jorōgumo?" he asked.

"No, there are no male jorōgumo. Our kind are female only, like the ningyo—the women-fish—of the distant sea. But I have the power to transform you into a yōkai of your own design."

Takashi thought for a time as he gazed into

Shiori's ocean-blue eyes.

"Will you accept my offer?" she implored. "Could you learn to love all that I am? I can never be a simple farmer's wife, but I will care for you and stay by your side—as any good wife should—until the end, should it ever come."

Takashi touched her cheek without hesitation, marvelling at her beauty. "You are my Silk Maiden, and I would love to spend all the days of my life with you, Shiori, in whatever form that takes, and for however long that may be."

A single tear etched its way down Shiori's moon-pale face. "Then let our adventure begin." The beautiful yōkai encouraged Takashi to embrace her. Then nuzzling affectionately against the confluence of his neck and shoulder, she sank her fangs into his throat, sampling but a taste of his blood, before injecting him with her eternal venom. Takashi held Shiori tight as pain lanced through him, racing through his veins like wildfire. Soon weakness overcame him, and moments later, a peaceful, tangible darkness claimed him.

When Takashi next awoke, he found himself cradled within a hammock of soft, glistening silk, suspended above the pit from immense amethyst stalactites on the cavern's ceiling. By his side Shiori lay against him, one arm over his chest, her hand resting upon his heart. Observing the nest about him with new eyes, everything seemed infinitely more detailed and beautiful. He could see glittering veins of turquoise and jade running through the cavern's walls, and the gargantuan gemstones reflected the trembling, dancing flames cast by the torches that burned in iron sconces on the cavern floor.

"Konbanwa, my love," said Shiori.

"Good evening to you, too," he replied. "I feel strange," Takashi admitted. "It seems as if all of my senses have been heightened."

"They are, Takashi-chan. You have died and passed through the gates of death to be reborn anew. You are now yōkai, like me. You'll be stronger, faster, and capable of feats only dreamed of by mortal men."

Takashi sighed, and relaxed, hope and happiness coursing through him as he pulled his Silk Maiden closer. "What an adventure, indeed," he exclaimed. "Tomorrow, I'd like to introduce you to my mother. She is in poor health and is not long for this world. She may live to see but a handful of summers more. And I would have her see me happy before her time comes."

Shiori tensed. "I have never ventured far from my nest, my love," she answered with trepidation. "But if it means so much to you, I will gladly do it. It has been too long since I had a mother to speak to and confide in. And I would give her what pride and comfort I can. The life of a jorōgumo is usually a lonely one."

"Then it's settled. Tomorrow, my mother gains a daughter, you shall gain a mother, and I, a beautiful wife."

Shiori smiled in the darkness, her fingers walking across his chest. "Before we travel, might we first find dinner, Takashi-chan? The turn of events this day has left me with an empty belly!"

Takashi laughed, his amusement filling the darkness. "Of course, my precious weaver. I couldn't very well deprive you of a meal twice, now, could I?

That would be most improper."

His yōkai bride's enchanting laughter joined his own, her fangs glinting in the firelight as they embraced. The union of their hearts and flesh as one—a tangle of ebony locks, red lips, and moon-pale limbs—in a majestic bed of soft white silk.

49

ABOUT THE AUTHOR

ZOEY XOLTON is an Australian Romance Author. "Romance of every flavour!" is her motto. She likes to daydream, and write stories about the beautiful and improbable, the dark and fantastical, as well as the adventurous and utterly romantic!

Zoey has been published in over one-hundred bestselling anthologies to date, and is a proud member of the Romance Writers of Australia.

She prays you enjoy, and fall in love with the deliciously tempting tales, and characters that she brings into the world. Writing is Zoey's guilty pleasure…perhaps reading her tales will become yours?

Bibliography

Bad Romance, Black Hare Press, 2020
Coffins & Dragons, Dragon Soul Press, 2019
Darkly Ever After, Blood Song Books, 2020
Divinity, Iron Faerie Publishing, 2019

Fable, Iron Faerie Publishing, 2019
Falling for Shifters, Dangerous Words
Publishing, 2020
First Love, Dragon Soul Press, 2019
Galactic Goddesses, Fantasia Divinity Publishing,
2019
Golden Desires, Blood Song Books, 2020
Key to the Kingdom, Black Hare Press, 2020
Midsummer Night Shifts, Dangerous Words
Publishing, 2020
Midnight Masquerade, Fantasia Divinity
Publishing, 2018
Of Fables & Fae, Pauline Creeden Anthologies,
2020
Sea of Secrets, Dragon Soul Press, 2019
Spring's Blessing, Fantasia Divinity Publishing,
2019
Summer's Splash, Fantasia Divinity Publishing,
2019
Twenty Twenty, Black Hare Press, 2020
What If?, Black Hare Press, 2019

Connect

Website: www.zoeyxolton.com

Amazon: www.amazon.com/author/zoeyxolton

ABOUT THE PUBLISHER

BLACK HARE PRESS is a small, independent publisher based in Melbourne, Australia.

Founded in 2018, our aim has always been to champion emerging authors from all around the globe and offer opportunities for them to participate in speculative fiction and horror short story anthologies.

Connect

Website: *www.blackharepress.com*

Twitter: *@BlackHarePress*

9 781925 809756